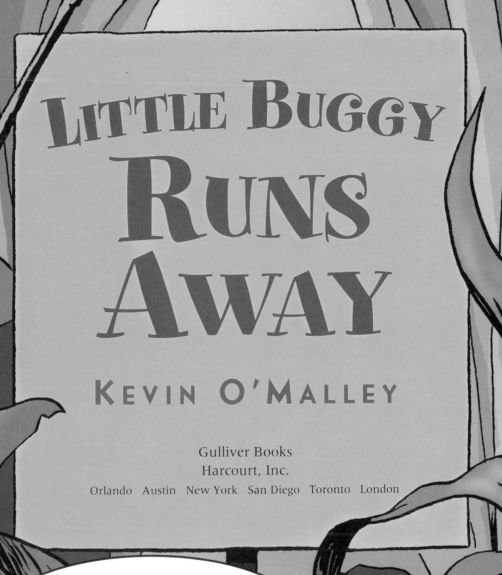

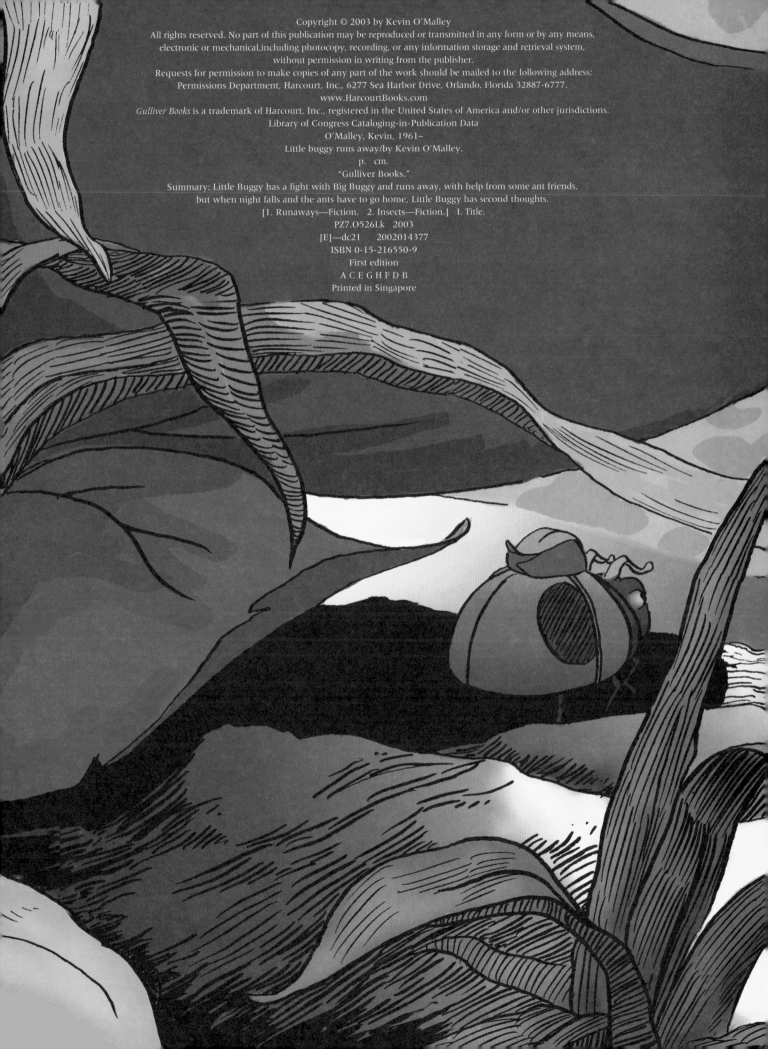

Requests for permission to make copies of any part of the work should be mailed to the following address:
Permissions Department, Harcourt, Inc., 6277 Sea Harbor Drive, Orlando, Florida 32887-6777.
www.HarcourtBooks.com
Gulliver Books is a trademark of Harcourt, Inc., registered in the United States of America and/or other jurisdictions.
Library of Congress Cataloging-in-Publication Data
O'Malley, Kevin, 1961–
Little buggy runs away/by Kevin O'Malley.
p.   cm.
"Gulliver Books."
Summary: Little Buggy has a fight with Big Buggy and runs away, with help from some ant friends,
but when night falls and the ants have to go home, Little Buggy has second thoughts.
[1. Runaways—Fiction.   2. Insects—Fiction.]   I. Title.
PZ7.O526Lk   2003
[E]—dc21   2002014377
ISBN 0-15-216550-9
First edition
A C E G H F D B
Printed in Singapore

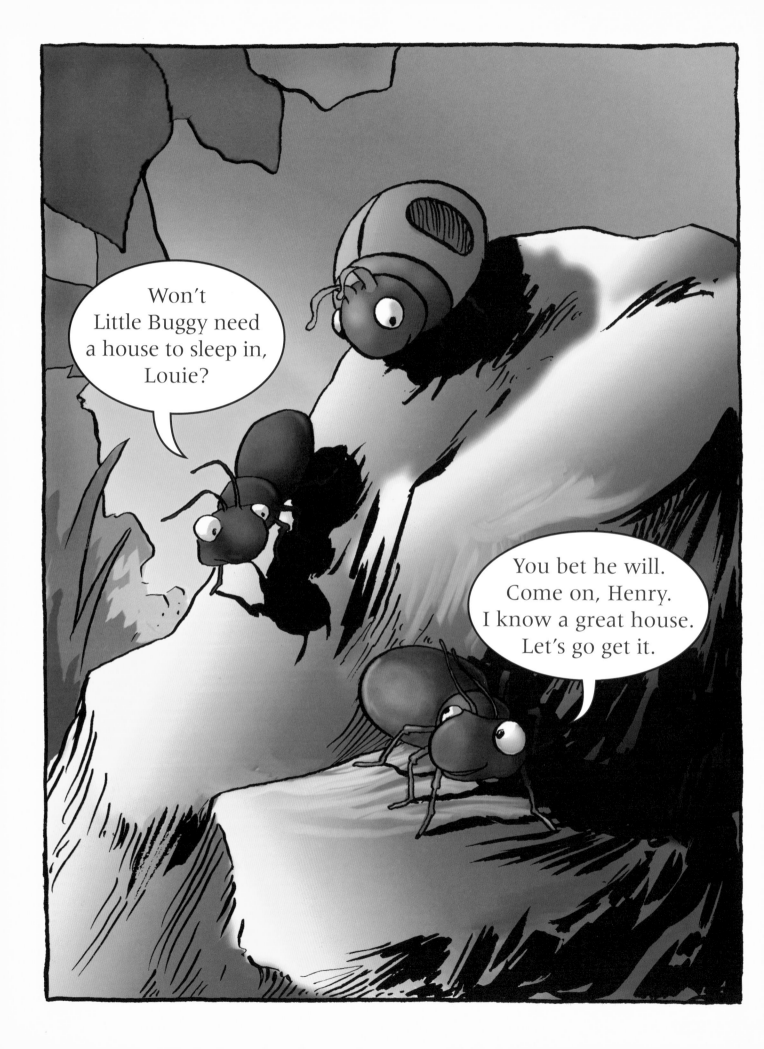

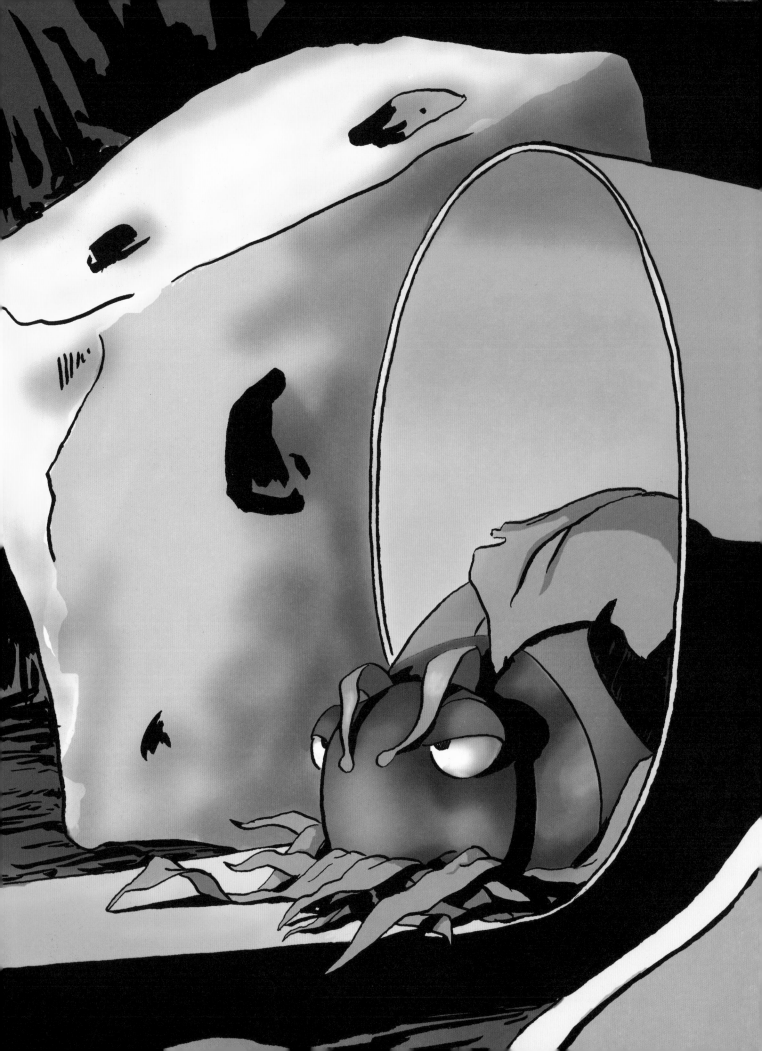